GOD'S WONDERFUL
COLORING
BOOK

ENDANGERED CREATURES

1 The *white rhinoceros* is the largest land animal in the world apart from the elephant. It lives peacefully on the African savannahs, grazing on grass. Although it has grey skin, this rhinoceros may look reddish-brown if it has been wallowing in mud. There are hardly any white rhinos left in the world.

2

The *giant panda* is related to both bears and racoons. It lives in bamboo forests in the mountains of central China and is now very rare (even though people are trying to protect it). The panda must eat a huge amount of bamboo each day to stay alive and its front paws are specially shaped for holding bamboo shoots.

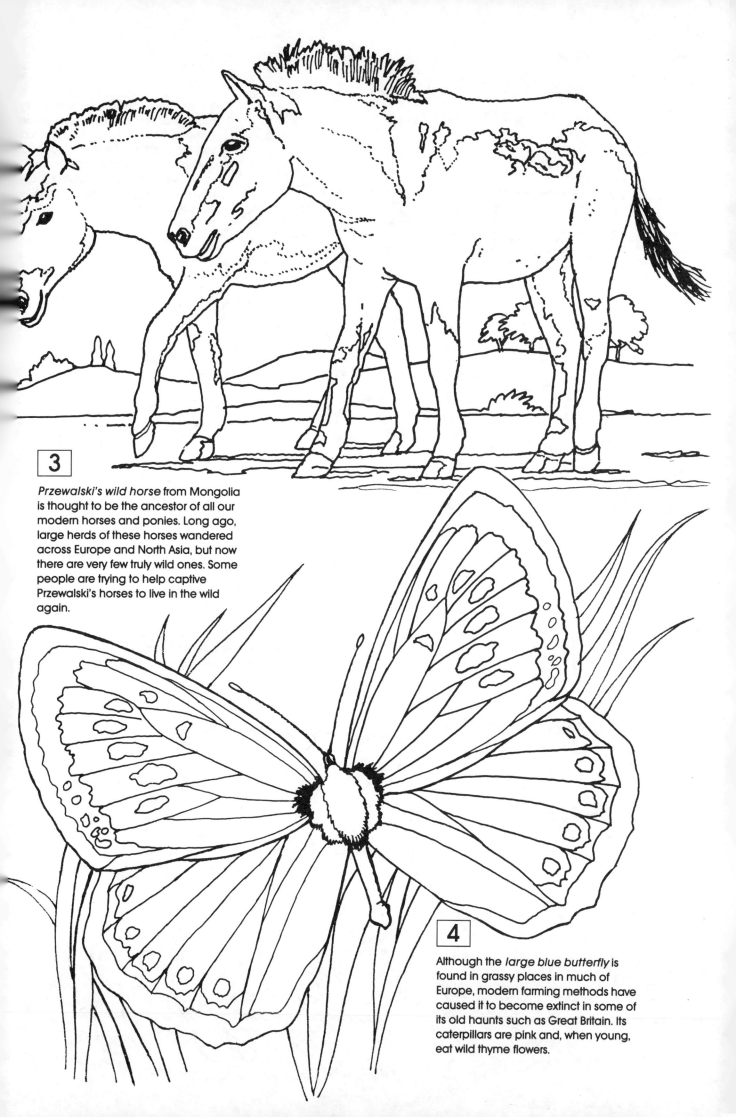

3

Przewalski's wild horse from Mongolia is thought to be the ancestor of all our modern horses and ponies. Long ago, large herds of these horses wandered across Europe and North Asia, but now there are very few truly wild ones. Some people are trying to help captive Przewalski's horses to live in the wild again.

4

Although the *large blue butterfly* is found in grassy places in much of Europe, modern farming methods have caused it to become extinct in some of its old haunts such as Great Britain. Its caterpillars are pink and, when young, eat wild thyme flowers.

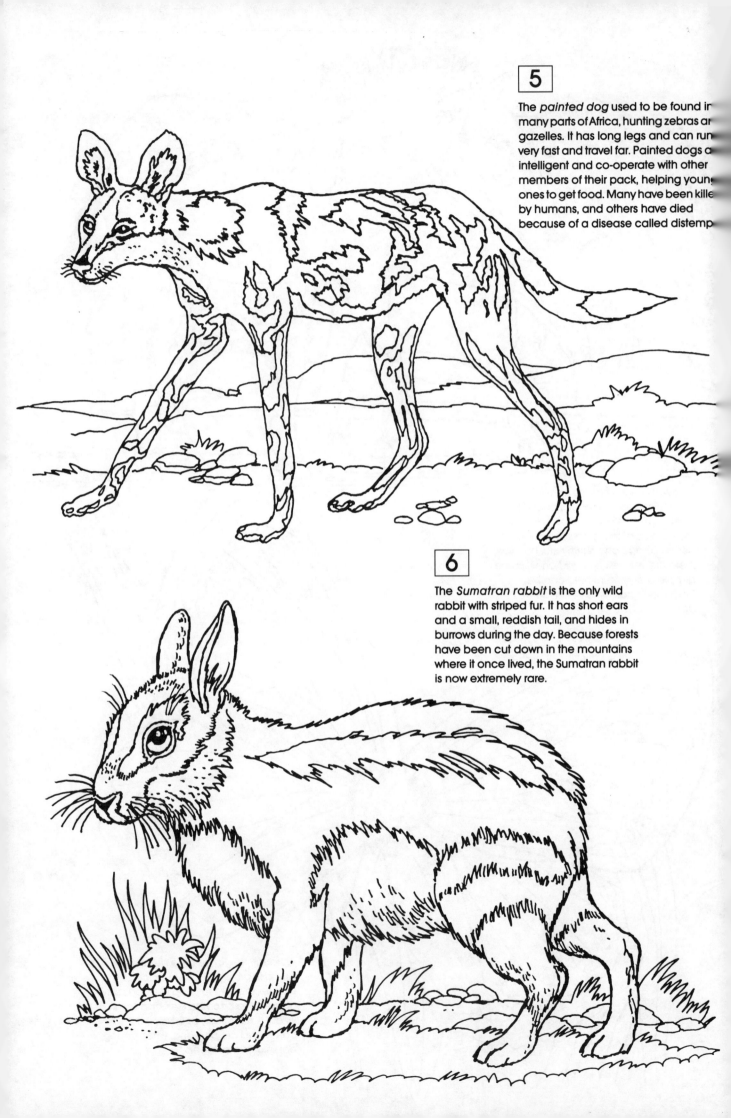

5

The *painted dog* used to be found in many parts of Africa, hunting zebras and gazelles. It has long legs and can run very fast and travel far. Painted dogs are intelligent and co-operate with other members of their pack, helping young ones to get food. Many have been killed by humans, and others have died because of a disease called distemper.

6

The *Sumatran rabbit* is the only wild rabbit with striped fur. It has short ears and a small, reddish tail, and hides in burrows during the day. Because forests have been cut down in the mountains where it once lived, the Sumatran rabbit is now extremely rare.

7

The *mandrill* is a baboon which lives in groups in the forests of Cameroon and Gabon in Africa. The male is much larger than the female and has bright markings on its buttock pads and ridged snout, which get darker when it is excited! Mandrills spend most of their time on the ground but climb trees to sleep at night and to escape from their enemies—mainly leopards and humans.

8

The *aye-aye* is related to the monkey
family but, with its bushy tail, looks more
like a squirrel. It has a long middle finger
which it uses to pick insect grubs out of
tree bark. The aye-aye has big eyes to
see at night, and sleeps during the day
in a twig nest high in a tree. Only a few still
exist in nature reserves in Madagascar,
because the forests that they once lived
in have been destroyed.

9

The *Barbary leopard*, from north-west Africa, is in danger of dying out because it is hunted for its beautiful spotted coat. Like other leopards, it hunts all kinds of animals, often springing down on them from a tree. Leopards usually live on their own, except when the female has cubs.

10

The *kakapo*, or *owl parrot*, is an unusual
parrot from New Zealand. It lives on the
ground, eating moss, leaves and fruit at
night, and sleeping during the day.
Because it cannot fly, the kakapo is
easily killed by the rats and stoats which
have come to New Zealand and has
nearly become extinct.

11

The *red siskin* is a beautiful little finch which eats seeds and insects along the forest edges of Venezuela. It is in great danger of becoming extinct because so many are trapped to become cage birds in other countries. Red siskins are often cross-bred with canaries (which have a better song) to make bright red or bronze canaries.

12

The *puna rhea* is like a small ostrich. It is named after the puna moorland in the high mountains of the Andes. The male rhea mates with many females and then sits alone on the green eggs which they lay. There may be over 50 eggs in one nest! The puna rhea is a very fast runner but is nearly extinct because it is hunted for sport, and for its skin, meat and feathers.

13

The *resplendent quetzal* lives in tropical "cloud forests", high in South America. The male bird's beautiful tail feathers form a train up to 90cm (3ft) long in the breeding season, to attract a mate. Now the quetzal is threatened because so many have been captured for cage birds.

14

The *waldrapp*, or *hermit ibis*, used to be found in Europe, but now there are only a few left, in Turkey, Morocco and Algeria. They make twiggy nests on ledges of houses and cliffs, which some people are trying to protect. Waldrapps have been hurt by the pesticides used on the plains and marshes where they find their food.

15

The *lammergeyer*, or *bearded vulture*, is the rarest bird of prey in Europe, although it is also found in the mountains of Africa, India and Tibet. It has huge wings and soars high in the air, gracefully swooping and diving. The lammergeyer feeds on the bones of dead animals and on tortoises, cracking them open to get the marrow by dropping them on to flat rocks.

16

The *Western tragopan* is a kind of pheasant which lives in thick forests in the Himalayan mountains. The male has special skin on his head and chest which he puffs out when he is courting the female. This shy and beautiful bird is now very rare.

17

The *red-knee tarantula spider* lives in burrows in dry, sandy places in Mexico. It feeds mainly on insects, but is also called the "bird-eating spider" and eats other small creatures. Although this tarantula spider has very irritating hairs and a poisonous bite, it is sold as a pet, and so it may be endangered.

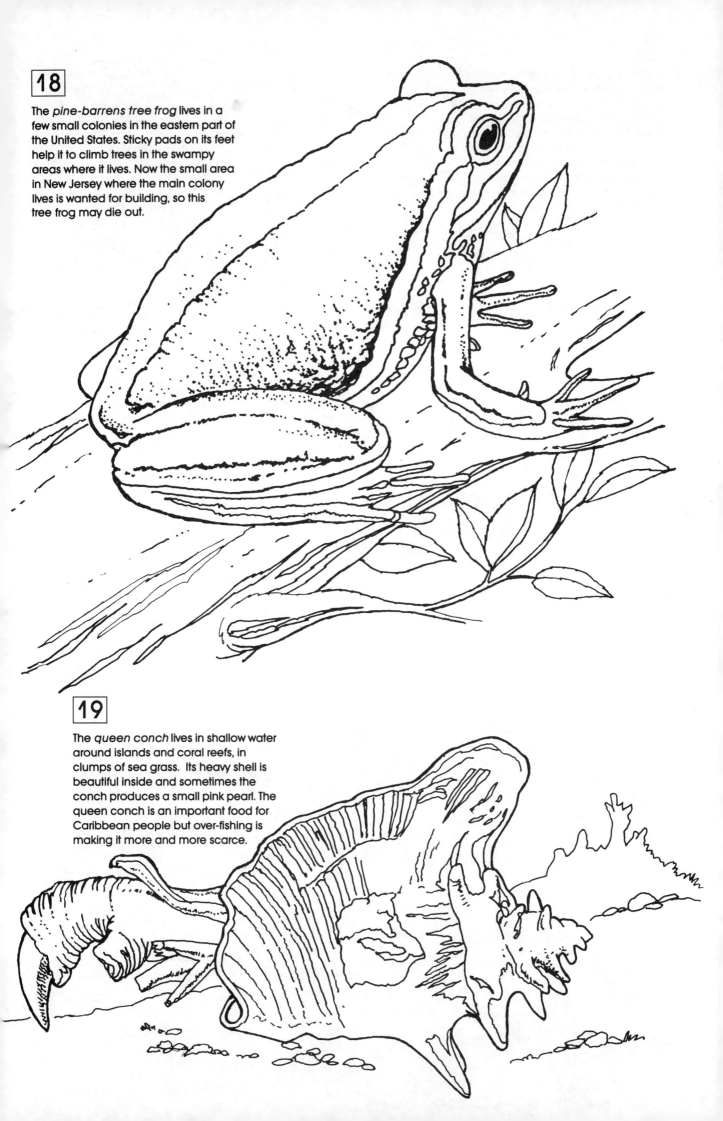

18

The *pine-barrens tree frog* lives in a few small colonies in the eastern part of the United States. Sticky pads on its feet help it to climb trees in the swampy areas where it lives. Now the small area in New Jersey where the main colony lives is wanted for building, so this tree frog may die out.

19

The *queen conch* lives in shallow water around islands and coral reefs, in clumps of sea grass. Its heavy shell is beautiful inside and sometimes the conch produces a small pink pearl. The queen conch is an important food for Caribbean people but over-fishing is making it more and more scarce.

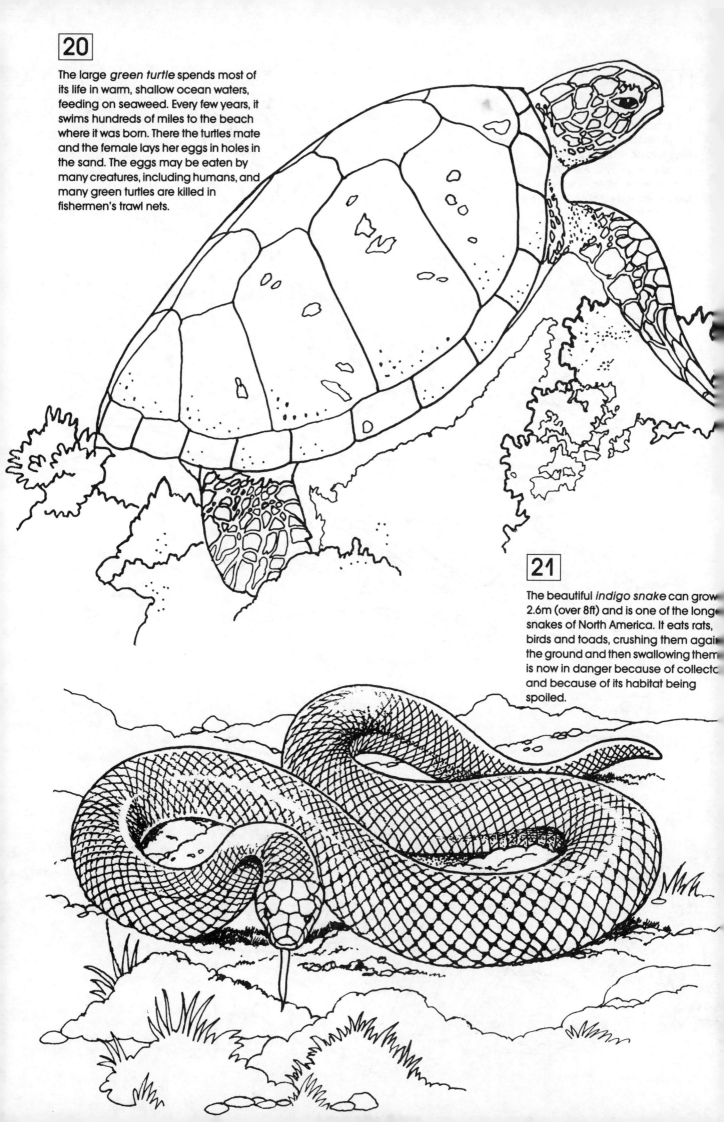

20

The large *green turtle* spends most of its life in warm, shallow ocean waters, feeding on seaweed. Every few years, it swims hundreds of miles to the beach where it was born. There the turtles mate and the female lays her eggs in holes in the sand. The eggs may be eaten by many creatures, including humans, and many green turtles are killed in fishermen's trawl nets.

21

The beautiful *indigo snake* can grow 2.6m (over 8ft) and is one of the long snakes of North America. It eats rats, birds and toads, crushing them again the ground and then swallowing them is now in danger because of collecto and because of its habitat being spoiled.

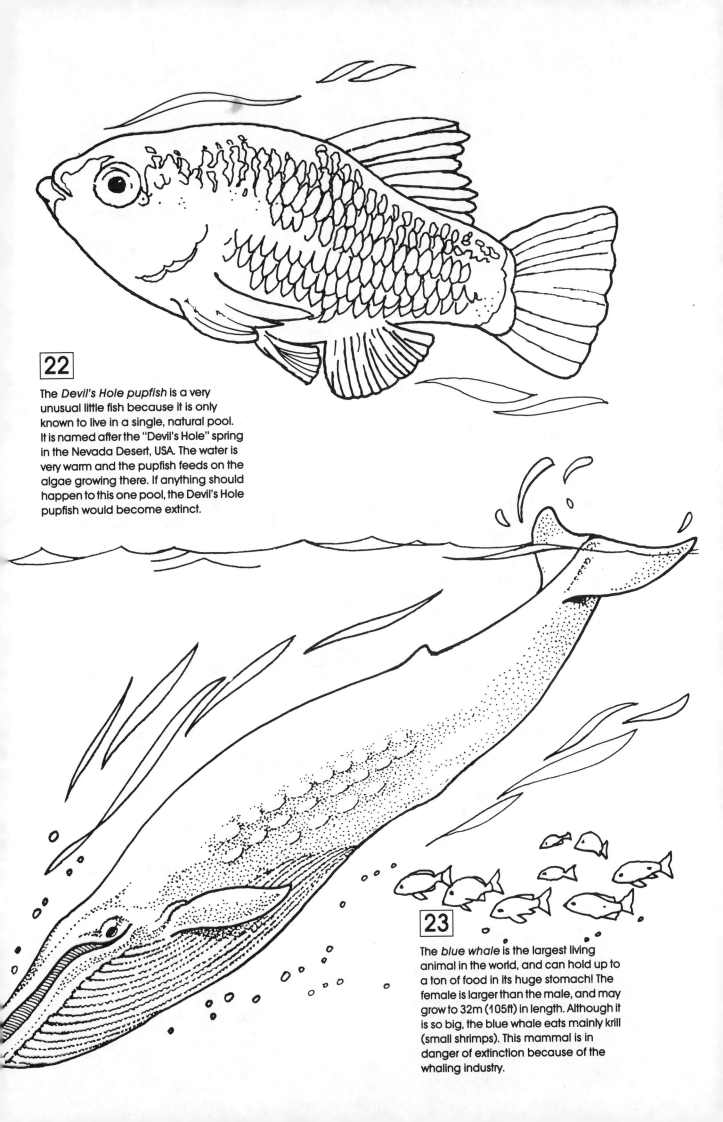

22

The *Devil's Hole pupfish* is a very
unusual little fish because it is only
known to live in a single, natural pool.
It is named after the "Devil's Hole" spring
in the Nevada Desert, USA. The water is
very warm and the pupfish feeds on the
algae growing there. If anything should
happen to this one pool, the Devil's Hole
pupfish would become extinct.

23

The *blue whale* is the largest living
animal in the world, and can hold up to
a ton of food in its huge stomach! The
female is larger than the male, and may
grow to 32m (105ft) in length. Although it
is so big, the blue whale eats mainly krill
(small shrimps). This mammal is in
danger of extinction because of the
whaling industry.

24

The *Indian gavial*, or *gharial*, is a river
crocodile with a long, slender snout. It
has over 100 sharp teeth, which it uses to
grab small fish and frogs from the water.
Like other crocodiles, the gavial has
been hunted for its scaly skin and is now
very rare.

GOD'S WONDERFUL WORLD
COLORING BOOK
ENDANGERED CREATURES

The birds, mammals, reptiles, and other creatures drawn come from all around the world. They show the wonder God's creation as they have such different shapes, sizes, and ways of life. But they have one sad thing in common—every one is in danger of dying out in places where it was once wild, or even of soon becoming extinct. Yet each of these animals is a precious part of our world, which can never be replaced.

Instead of taking care of the world as they were meant to do, people have often exploited the animal kingdom. When we act selfishly or thoughtlessly we often put animals at risk. Some creatures are endangered because people demand exotic skins, feathers, or ivory just to be in fashion. Others are captured as pets, but these may die in captivity. By over-hunting and fishing and through sheer carelessness, humans have nearly destroyed entire species of animals. And many of these creatures are also threatened because they no longer have enough room to live and feed.

It might not seem to matter much if a very tiny creature dies out. Yet the earth was created so that animals, fish, birds and insects, large and small, could live in a natural balance. Some species look alike, but each kind has a special part in our world. Even creatures which may not seem pretty or useful may be very valuable to people in ways that we don't yet understand.

We now know that when people chop down forests, use too many chemicals on the land or pollute water, our selfishness doesn't hurt just a few faraway animals, we also hurt ourselves—wherever we are. By being less selfish in the way we live and the way we treat our world, we can help these beautiful creatures *and* help ourselves as well.

Other Lion coloring books for you to collect:
BIRDS BUTTERFLIES FISH FLOWERS JUNGLES PETS SEASHORE WOODLANDS
DEEP SEA CREATURES

Published by
Lion Publishing Corporation
1705 Hubbard Avenue, Batavia
Illinois 60510, USA

ISBN 0 7459 2144 2

Illustrations copyright © 1991 Vic Mitchell
Copyright © 1991 Lion Publishing

First edition 1991

All rights reserved

Printed and bound in Malta

9 780745 9214

GOD'S WONDERFUL WORLD
COLORING BOOK

DEEP SEA CREATURES

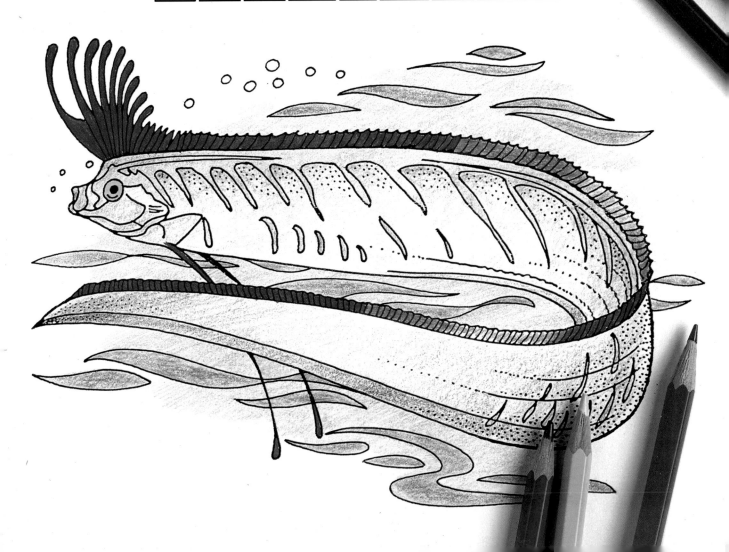